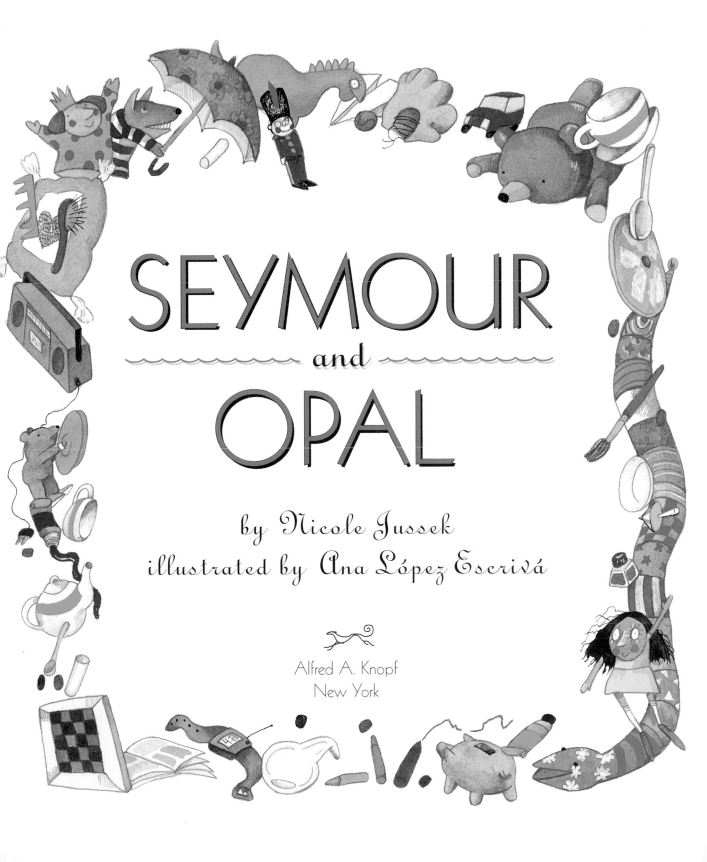

SEYMOUR
and
OPAL

by Nicole Jussek
illustrated by Ana López Escrivá

Alfred A. Knopf
New York

For Deborah Ann—the real Opal—
and for my parents —N. J.

For Andrés —A. L. E.

~~~~~~~~~~~~~~~~~~~~~~~~~~~~~~~~~~~

Text copyright © 1996 by Nicole Jussek.
Illustrations copyright © 1996 by Ana López Escrivá.
All rights reserved under International and Pan-American Copyright Conventions. Published in the United
States of America by Alfred A. Knopf, Inc., New York, and simultaneously in Canada by Random House of
Canada Limited, Toronto. Distributed by Random House, Inc., New York. Book design by Janet Pedersen.

Library of Congress Cataloging-in-Publication Data
Jussek, Nicole.
Seymour and Opal / by Nicole Jussek ; illustrated by Ana López Escrivá.
p. cm.
Summary: Every time his sister Opal passes through his room to get to her own, Seymour charges her a toll;
but Opal eventually teaches him a lesson.
ISBN 0-679-86722-8 (trade)
ISBN 0-679-96722-2 (lib. bdg.)
[1. Rabbits—Fiction. 2. Brothers and sisters—Fiction.] I. Escrivá, Ana López, ill. II. Title.
PZ7.966Se 1996
[E]—dc20 95-14564

Printed in Singapore

10 9 8 7 6 5 4 3 2

http://www.randomhouse.com/

SEYMOUR and OPAL
lived in a two-story house
with an avocado tree
on the front lawn.

Opal had to pass through Seymour's room to get into her own.

Opal was as happy as she could be, until one day when Seymour decided to charge a toll.

"Why?" asked Opal.

"Because," said Seymour.

Opal thought of telling Mother and Father.

"Don't even think," said Seymour, "of telling Mother and Father."

"Why?" asked Opal.

"Because," said Seymour.

Every time Opal went into her room, she had to give Seymour a nickel.

Seymour never forgot, and he grew very wealthy.

One Sunday after lunch, Opal's piggy bank was empty.

   Outside, it had begun to rain. Seymour watched
huge drops trickle down the windowpane. He
tossed a softball into the air and caught it with his
baseball glove. He looked at his tin soldiers, but
they just stood in a line and stared back at him.
He knocked at Opal's door.

"How about a game of marbles?" he asked.
"No, thanks," said Opal, who was busy
braiding her doll Ethel's hair.

Seymour went back to his room and counted the ants in his ant farm. Then he went downstairs to see what his mother and father were doing.

His mother was painting a portrait for art class.
Uncle Johnny had come to pose.

"What's the matter, my little dumpling?" she asked.

"Nothing," sighed Seymour.

Seymour went into the kitchen, where his
father was singing an aria and inventing a new
kind of pizza for supper.

Seymour went back to his room and peeped through the keyhole.

Opal had set up a science lab with test tubes and colored powders.

"Want to watch TV?" Seymour asked.

"No, thanks," said Opal. "I'm teaching Ethel how to make a rainbow."

Seymour set up a game of checkers
against himself. Then he knocked at
Opal's door.

"Want to come and splash in rain puddles in the garden?" he asked.

"No, thanks," said Opal. "Three good fairies have come to tea."

Opal had set a lovely table with her dolly china and tablecloth, and she was filling Ethel's cup.

After a while Seymour wanted to listen to the radio in Opal's room.

"Not now!" shouted Opal from a tepee made of two chairs and a blanket. "White Bear and I are threading bead necklaces for him to take back to his tribe."

"I'll give you a nickel if you let me play," said Seymour.

"No, thanks," said Opal.

"Two nickels?" said Seymour, but Opal said, "Nope."

"Why?" asked Seymour.

"Because," said Opal.

"I'll let you walk through my room any-time you want," said Seymour. "For free."

"And can I borrow your walkie-talkie wrist-watch set for my expedition to the North Pole tomorrow after school?" asked Opal.

"If you insist," said Seymour.

And she did.

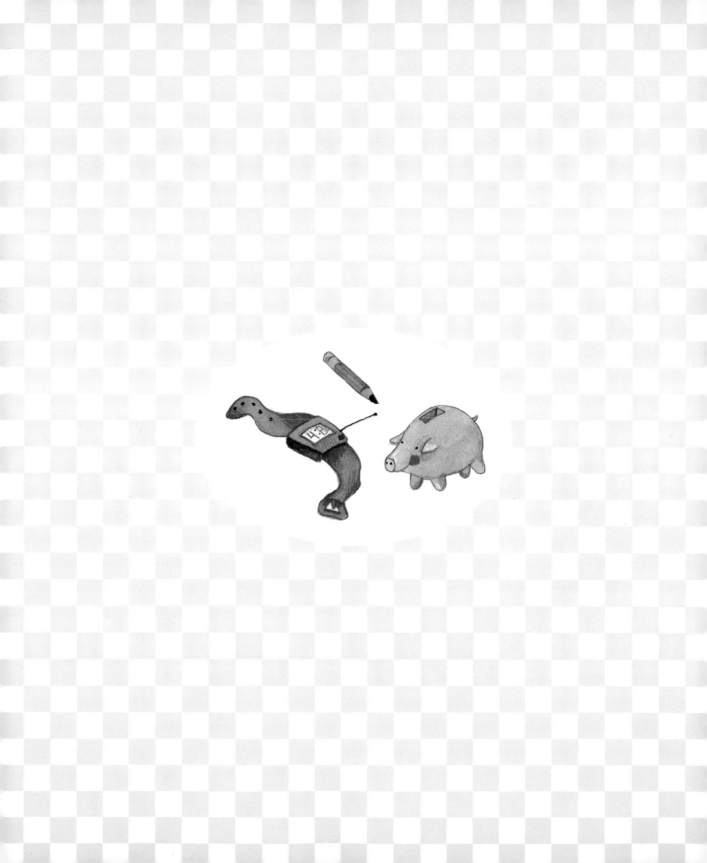